Chicken
Tricken

by Dawn McNiff and Karl West

FRANKLIN WATTS
LONDON • SYDNEY

This story is based on the traditional fairy tale,
Chicken Licken, but with a new twist.
You can read the original story in
Must Know Stories. Can you make
up your own twist for the story?

Franklin Watts
First published in Great Britain in 2016
by the Watts Publishing Group

ISBN 978 1 4451 4788 8 (hbk)
ISBN 978 1 4451 4790 1 (pbk)
ISBN 978 1 4451 4789 5 (library ebook)

Series Editor: Melanie Palmer
Series Advisor: Catherine Glavina
Series Designer: Peter Scoulding
Cover Designer: Cathryn Gilbert

Printed in China

Franklin Watts
An imprint of
Hachette Children's Group
Part of The Watts Publishing Group
Carmelite House
50 Victoria Embankment
London EC4Y 0DZ

An Hachette UK Company
www.hachette.co.uk

www.franklinwatts.co.uk

MIX
Paper from
responsible sources
FSC® C104740
FSC
www.fsc.org

Chicken Tricken was clever, and
very good at tricks.

Tricks

4   99 Water Tricks

He loved tricking Ducky Lucky and Goosey Loosey.

Then one day some acorns fell.

"Look out, the sky is falling down!"

Chicken Tricken lied.

"Quick, follow me!" He led Ducky

Lucky and Goosey Loosey to a barn.

Then he flew back to the
farmyard, and ate up **ALL**
the corn by himself.

Chicken Tricken played this trick a lot. But he was soon bored of corn. "I want nicer dinners," he said. "And I want to do better tricks!"

So he flew out of the farmyard
and into the woods.

There he met Little Red Riding
Hood with a basket of iced buns.
"Ooh, I'll trick her and get those!"
thought Chicken Tricken.

"Look out, the wolf is coming,"
he squawked. "Quick, follow me!"

Little Red Riding Hood dropped her basket and followed him out of the woods, screaming.

Quick as he could, Chicken Tricken flew back and ate all the buns. "Yum, yum!" he clucked.

He came to a cottage. Goldilocks was inside eating porridge. "Time for another trick," he thought.

"Look out, the three bears are coming!" squawked Chicken Tricken. "Quick, follow me!"

Goldilocks followed him out of the wood, howling.

Chicken Tricken zoomed back to the cottage. He ate all the creamy porridge in the bowls. "Delicious," he clucked.

Next he came across a gingerbread house. Hansel and Gretel were nibbling the roof.

"Look out, the witch is coming!" fibbed Chicken Tricken. "Quick, follow me!"

Hansel and Gretel followed him
out of the woods in a panic.

Chicken Tricken flew back and ate the **WHOLE** gingerbread house, all by himself.

Now his tummy was bursting.
He was too fat to fly so he lay
down for a rest ...

... but soon he was woken up by a furry nose sniffing him.

"Look out! The wolf, the three bears and the witch are coming!" barked the furry stranger.

"They're cross with you, because they can't find Little Red Riding Hood, Goldilocks, or Hansel and Gretel in the woods. Quick, follow me!"

Chicken Tricken followed him.
"Hide in this pie!" said the furry
stranger.

MENU
Chicken
Chicken pie
Chicken pizza

Fat
Chicken
Pie

"Good idea," said Chicken Tricken, hopping inside. There he stayed...

...until he saw his chance to escape. He had TRICKED Foxy Loxy too!

Recipes for Chicken

Because Chicken Tricken really
was clever, and very good at tricks.

Puzzle 1

Put these pictures in the correct order.
Which event do you think is most important?
Now try writing the story in your own words!

Puzzle 2

Choose the correct speech bubbles for each character. Can you think of any others? Turn over to find the answers.

Answers

Puzzle 1

The correct order is: 1b, 2e, 3f, 4a, 5c, 6d

Puzzle 2

Chicken Tricken: 3, 5

Goosey Loosey: 2, 6

Foxy Loxy: 1, 4

Look out for more Hopscotch Twisty Tales

The Ninjabread Man
ISBN 978 1 4451 3964 7

The Boy Who Cried Sheep!
ISBN 978 1 4451 4292 0

Thumbelina Thinks Big
ISBN 978 1 4451 4296 8

**Move versus the
Enormous Turnip**
ISBN 978 1 4451 4300 2

Big Pancacke to the Rescue
ISBN 978 1 4451 4303 3

Little Red Hen's Great Escape
ISBN 978 1 4451 4305 7

The Lovely Duckling
ISBN 978 1 4451 1633 4

**Hansel and Gretel
and the Green Witch**
ISBN 978 1 4451 1634 1

The Emperor's New Kit
ISBN 978 1 4451 1635 8

**Rapunzel and the
Prince of Pop**
ISBN 978 1 4451 1636 5

**Dick Whittington
Gets on his Bike**
ISBN 978 1 4451 1637 2

**The Pied Piper and
the Wrong Song**
ISBN 978 1 4451 1638 9

**The Princess and the
Frozen Peas**
ISBN 978 1 4451 0675 5

Snow White Sees the Light
ISBN 978 1 4451 0676 2

**The Elves and the
Trendy Shoes**
ISBN 978 1 4451 0678 6

The Three Frilly Goats Fluff
ISBN 978 1 4451 0677 9

Princess Frog
ISBN 978 1 4451 0679 3

Rumpled Stilton Skin
ISBN 978 1 4451 0680 9

Jack and the Bean Pie
ISBN 978 1 4451 0182 8

**Brownilocks and the Three Bowls
of Cornflakes**
ISBN 978 1 4451 0183 5

Cinderella's Big Foot
ISBN 978 1 4451 0184 2

Little Bad Riding Hood
ISBN 978 1 4451 0185 9

**Sleeping Beauty –
100 Years Later**
ISBN 978 1 4451 0186 6

**The Three Little Pigs &
the New Neighbour**
ISBN 978 1 4451 0181 1

For more Hopscotch books go to:
www.franklinwatts.co.uk